ADVANCE PRAISE FOR
THE LIGHTKEEPER'S DAUGHTER

"Colleen Coble has long been a favorite storyteller of mine. I love the way she weaves intrigue and God's love in to a story chock-full of carefully crafted characters. If you're looking for an awesome writer— I highly recommend her!"

—Tracie Peterson, best-selling author of
Dawn's Prelude, Song of Alaska series

"Colleen delivers a heart-warming romance—and plot twists that will keep you guessing until the final page! Perhaps best of all, her novels call us to a deeper, richer faith."

—Tamera Alexander, best-selling author of
The Inheritance and *Beyond this Moment*

"*The Lightkeeper's Daughter* is a maze of twists and turns with an opening that grabs the reader instantly. With so many red herrings, the villain caught me by surprise."

—Lauraine Snelling, best-selling
author of *A Measure of Mercy*

THE
LIGHTKEEPER'S
DAUGHTER

A Mercy Falls Novel

Colleen Coble

THOMAS NELSON
Since 1798

NASHVILLE   DALLAS   MEXICO CITY   RIO DE JANEIRO

Published in Nashville, Tennessee, by Thomas Nelson. Thomas Nelson is a registered trademark of Thomas Nelson, Inc.

Thomas Nelson, Inc., titles may be purchased in bulk for educational, business, fund-raising, or sales promotional use. For information, please e-mail SpecialMarkets@ThomasNelson.com.

Publisher's note: This novel is a work of fiction. Names, characters, places, and incidents are either products of the author's imagination or used fictitiously. All characters are fictional, and any similarity to people, living or dead, is purely coincidental.

KING JAMES VERSION is in the public domain and does not require permission.

Library of Congress Cataloging-in-Publication Data

Coble, Colleen.
 The lightkeeper's daughter : a Mercy Falls novel / Colleen Coble.
  p. cm.
 ISBN 978-1-59554-267-0 (softcover : alk. paper)
  1. Nannies—Fiction. 2. California—History—1850–1950—Fiction. 3. Domestic fiction. I. Title.
PS3553.O2285L54 2010
813'.54—dc22   2009045066

Printed in the United States of America

10 11 12 13 RRD 6 5 4 3 2